Dinosaur Adventures

Written by Fran Bromage

Miles Kelly

First published in 2018 by Miles Kelly Publishing Ltd
Harding's Barn, Bardfield End Green, Thaxted, Essex, CM6 3PX, UK

Copyright © Miles Kelly Publishing Ltd 2018

This edition printed 2018

2 4 6 8 10 9 7 5 3

Publishing Director Belinda Gallagher
Creative Director Jo Cowan
Editorial Director Rosie Neave
Senior Editor Fran Bromage
Senior Designer Rob Hale
Production Elizabeth Collins, Jennifer Brunwin-Jones
Reprographics Stephan Davis, Jennifer Cozens
Assets Lorraine King

ISBN 978-1-78617-521-2

Printed in China

British Library Cataloguing-in-Publication Data
A catalogue record for this book is available from the British Library

ACKNOWLEDGEMENTS
The publishers would like to thank the following artists who have contributed to this book:
Advocate Art: Louise Forshaw (Velociraptor); The Bright Agency: Chris Jevons (T rex),
Richard Watson (Diplodocus), Tom Heard (Ankylosaurus)

Made with paper from a sustainable forest

www.mileskelly.net

T rex

The big scare

Long, long ago there lived
a dinosaur called Rex.

"When I grow up, I'm going to
be the **biggest**, **scariest**,
noisiest dinosaur ever,"
he roared.

RROOOOAAARRR!

4

"I'll be just like my mum, and we're **not afraid** of anything!" said the young Tyrannosaurus rex.

5

Rex didn't have many friends.

He was just too big, too scary and too noisy to play with.

6

One day Rex was stomping through the forest when he **scared** a Troodon called Travis.

RRROOOAAARRR!

"Aah! Don't DO that, Rex!" cried Travis.

"I can do what I want. I'm going to be the **biggest, scariest, noisiest** dinosaur ever!" roared Rex.

7

"Aah! cried Trudi. "Stop **doing** that Rex or you might be sorry."

"I'm not afraid of anything!" roared Rex. "I'm going to be the **biggest**, scariest, noisiest dinosaur ever!"

9

Everyone was **very tired** of Rex scaring them.

So, the next day Travis and the other Troodons came up with a plan.

10

Travis went to find Rex in the forest and said:

"You won't be the biggest dinosaur ever. My dad says there are **lots of dinosaurs** bigger than you!

Rex was furious! So he chased after Travis, roaring loudly.

Travis **raced through the trees** and led Rex down towards the lake.

"I can still be the scariest, noisiest dinosaur!" roared Rex. "I'm **not afraid** of anything!"

12

Rex skidded to a halt by a group of Troodons who were **gathered in a circle.**

"Look what we found," they said, showing Rex some **bright white things.**

"What ARE they?" whispered Rex.

The **bright white** things were flowers, but few dinosaurs had ever seen them before.

BBBUZZZZ!

Suddenly, a low humming sound came from inside the flower.

14

"Aaahhh!" bellowed Rex, backing away.

"Buzzzz, buzz!" said the flower again,
and Rex ran shrieking into the trees.

15

"Look!" said Travis. "It's just a little stripy thing," and a **buzzy bee** crawled out of the flower.

"Rex was so scared! We're **not afraid of him** now," laughed the Troodons.

BBBUZZZZ!

16

But Rex was too far away to hear them. He ran and ran and ran until he found Trudi Triceratops.

Rex told Trudi all about the **buzzing white** things.

So Trudi decided to go to the lake and **see for herself.** 17

Rex watched from **behind a rock**
as Trudi walked closer to the lake.

He could see the **white flowers**
and the stripy buzzing things.
"What are they?" Rex whispered.

18

"Aaah, these are flowers!" said the wise, old Triceratops. "You'll see many more of these as the world begins to change."

"And these buzzy things are bees. They help the flowers to grow. There's nothing scary here," said Trudi.

BBBUZZZZ!

19

Rex sat quietly on a rock looking around him.

"But I WAS scared," said Rex to himself. "And I'm not supposed to be afraid of anything!"

"Yeah!" shouted Travis popping up behind Rex. "Terrible T rex is scared of flowers. Ha, ha!"

21

"Everyone is scared of something," said Trudi, moving closer. "But it isn't nice to be teased about it."

"But Rex teased us all the time," replied Travis. "And he was always scaring us with his roaring."

22

Suddenly, a **deafening noise** rocked the lake. It sounded just like a giant horn!

ARRR!

"Waaaaaaaaah! What was that?" cried Travis, as he leapt into Rex's arms.

23

Seconds later, Piper the Parasaurolophus appeared out of the water and blew her head crest again.

BBBWWWAAARRR!

"Ha, ha! It's only Piper," laughed Rex putting Travis down. "You were **really scared**."

"So were you!" shouted Travis over the noise. "But everyone's scared of something!"

25

"So I'll never be the **biggest, scariest** or **noisiest** dinosaur," sighed Rex. "I'm scared of flowers, bees and loud noises!"

"But Rex, we like you even more because of that!" said the others, and everyone laughed.

Diplodocus

The dippy idea

There was once a **huge and hungry** Diplodocus called Dora.

Dora often had lots of **dippy ideas** and was easily confused.

28

'Hmm... my favourite leaves are on that side of the tree,' she thought, one day.

'So I'll stand here and twist my neck like this to reach them!'

29

"Dora! You nearly **stepped on me!**" shouted a small Ornitholestes. "Head over there will you?"

"But my head IS over there," Dora replied, confused.

But before Dora could move away, an old Diplodocus appeared.

"Sssh! There's an Allosaurus about!" he hissed.

31

Dora made herself as **small as possible** and hid behind the nearest tree.

32

She watched as the herd swung their **enormous necks** and tails at the Allosaurus to scare them off.

33

After the fight **everyone was hungry**, but they also wanted to think of new ways to **scare off** the Allosaurus.

34

The Diplodocus were tired of all the **neck-swinging** and having their meals interrupted.

"We could disguise ourselves... as trees," suggested Dora, "with leaves on our heads!"

35

But no one took Dora seriously, so she **wandered off** on her own.

Deeper in the forest, Dora spotted a **Stegosaurus** frightening off another Allosaurus.

"You did it!" said Dora, strolling over to the smiling Stegosaurus called Peggy.

"I wish I had amazing armoured plates on my back," Dora sighed.

37

Peggy offered to help Dora make her own armour with mud and palm leaves.

"This is a great idea!" smiled Dora. "We'll all look so fierce – no Allosaurus will dare to come near us!"

But everyone laughed at Dora's idea and went back to eating leaves.

39

Poor Dora **felt sad** as she wandered down to the rocky shore to wash off her disguise.

"Never mind," said Peggy. "You'll think of something else."

"Er, Peggy?" whispered Dora. "What's that in the water?"

"Try it and see," said Pete.

So Dora found some reeds. 'These will help me breathe!' she thought, and she **dived right in!**

'What a good way to hide,' thought Dora. 'We could all fit down here.'

"And there's food!" said Dora, trying a big clump of seaweed.

She didn't see the Allosaurus had returned. And she didn't see Peggy trying to warn her.

46

"Peggy! I've got the
best idea," said Dora.
"I think we should...
wooooaaah!"

47

As Dora staggered out of the sea, she fell into a huge **puddle of mud**.

She was covered in thick, drippy black slime. The reeds, leaves and seaweed stuck out at all angles.

The Allosaurus had never seen anything so **terrifying** in all their lives!

49

"Well done Dora!" said another Diplodocus. "Your **dippy idea** wasn't so silly after all!"

50

Velociraptor

The speedy tale

Millions of years ago, there lived a Velociraptor called Vicky.

52

Vicky was super-speedy. Everywhere she went, she went in a rush.

"Got to go! Can't stop!" she'd shout, ignoring her baby brothers and sisters.

53

When Vicky's family was **ready to hunt**, no one could find her.

"I'll see if I can **catch her**," said Vicky's friend, Gal.

55

Gal, a Gallimimus, was the only dinosaur **fast enough** to keep up with Vicky.

"Vicky!" called Gal when he spotted her. "Your family is leaving..." But Vicky was off again.

56

Much later, Vicky
finally **slowed down.**

She looked around her. The forest
was **empty.** "Where is everyone?"
Vicky said out loud.

"They've gone," said an old voice, and an **ancient Protoceratops** limped into view. "I saw them go that way..." And Vicky was off again.

But she sped straight into a trap.

WAAAAAH!

That sneaky Protoceratops had sent Vicky straight over a cliff!

"You won't be eating any of my family tonight," **chuckled** the Protoceratops, peering down at Vicky.

As the old dinosaur ambled away, Gal tried to calm Vicky down.

"Stop flapping!" he shouted over the cliff.

61

But once at the top, Vicky sped off again. "I saw my family! I need to go!" she told Gal.

"There's a shortcut through here," she yelled, and Vicky ran...

63

But as she headed deeper into the jungle, Vicky **raced into trouble** again!

The vines and creepers quickly trapped her.

65

"Stop rushing!" said Gal, when he finally found her. "You're running into trouble at every turn."

66

Gal helped Vicky escape and led her to a hiding place near the slimy swamp.

"We'll trap the Tarbosaurus in the swamp," said Gal. "Keep shouting so they come closer."

67

"Why?" asked Vicky.
"We could just run."

"But we don't want to lead those two pea-brains straight to your family," replied Gal.

Both Tarbosaurus were soon **totally tied up** and stuck in the swamp.

69

A few moments later, Vicky and Gal **emerged** from the jungle.

They saw Vicky's family up on the hill. She was **excited** to see them again.

70

"Quietly and slowly," said Gal, "or we'll scare away the Protoceratops."

Vicky felt so grateful that Gal had taken the time to help her.

"Being fast is fun," she told the baby Velociraptors.

"But it's important to slow down, so you don't run into trouble."

72

Ankylosaurus

The clumsy club

Once upon a time there was an Ankylosaurus called Archie.

Archie was a tough-looking dinosaur, but he was ever so shy and ever so clumsy.

74

Archie had a huge club
at the end of his tail.

It seemed to do the
exact opposite of what
he wanted it to do.

75

When Archie walked, his club **swiped** from side to side.

He often **destroyed** things just by wandering past them.

So Archie spent a lot of time saying **SORRY** to other dinosaurs.

His club was always getting him into trouble.

WHOOOOSH!

77

"Watch your club!" grumbled an old Edmontonia. "I don't know why you've got one, if you can't control it."

78

Archie's best friend was a Styracosaurus called Stu.

But even with Stu about Archie was still **left out** of games.

"Stu! Come and play hide and seek," shouted an Ornithomimus called Olivia, one afternoon.

"HE can't play though," added Olivia, pointing to Archie. "He'll **knock** half the forest down before we've had time to hide."

It made Archie feel sad, but he told Stu to go and play anyway.

Archie stood and watched as all the other dinosaurs ran off to hide.

81

"Can I at least help you find them?" Archie asked Olivia, as he lumbered up to her.

"...18, 19, 20. Coming!" she shouted. "Oh, I suppose so," she replied, "just try to be quiet."

82

But suddenly Archie **spotted** a dinosaur who wasn't part of the game. "Olivia!" he shouted.

"Ssssh!" she replied crossly. "T REX!" hissed Archie.

83

"T REEEEEX!" shrieked Olivia, as she **overtook** Archie and sped towards a nearby cave.

Archie could see the other dinosaurs already **hiding in the cave.**

84

Stu was waiting for him, but was Archie going to get there in time?

Suddenly there was a **thundering roar** and the ground began to shake.

Archie wondered what he'd hit with his club this time. But when he looked behind him the sky was filling with smoke.

As the volcano shot
fiery balls of lava into
the air, Archie still
hadn't reached the cave.

Everyone else ducked
inside just as a
rumbling rockfall filled
the cave entrance.

87

Archie huddled close to the cave. As the eruption finished he started pushing at the rocks.

"I - can't - shift - any of them," he grunted.

88

"Try harder!" shouted Stu from inside the cave. "We can only move the little ones in here."

Olivia squeezed her head into the small gap Stu was making.

"use your club, Archie," suggested Olivia.

"I'll hurt someone," said Archie. "I always break something with it."

"Hurry Archie!" shouted Olivia. "T rex is back!"

90

"Just give your tail a swish and try. Please?" called Stu. So Archie started to spin...

91

Archie's club **slammed** into the fallen rocks. Small trees and boulders were caught up in his whirling and T rex was **knocked out** cold!

92

As Archie slowed to a stop, he saw the rocks around the cave had shifted.

"Well done Archie!" shouted the dinosaurs from inside the cave.

"Thanks Archie," whispered each dinosaur as they **tiptoed over T rex** to leave the cave.

"You took on a T rex with your tail?" whispered a small Edmontonia. "Amazing!"

Archie suddenly felt very proud of his club.

95

Archie was soon part of everyone's games and found he was especially good at rock-ball! "Archie's club is awesome!" laughed Olivia.